An Imprint of Starfish Bay Publishing
www.starfishbaypublishing.com
STARFISH BAY is a trademark of Starfish Bay Publishing Pty Ltd.

SAILING TO AMERICA

This edition © Starfish Bay Publishing, 2018
Printed and bound in China by Beijing Shangtang Print & Packaging Co., Ltd.
11 Tengren Road, Niulanshan Town, Shunyi District, Beijing, China
ISBN 978-1-76036-046-7

Die Reise nach Amerika © Dressler Verlag – Imprint Ellermann, Hamburg 2017.
Published by agreement with Dressler Verlag GmbH, Hamburg, Germany.
Translated by David-Henry Wilson

ROBERT GERNHARDT · PHILIP WAECHTER

SAILING TO AMERICA

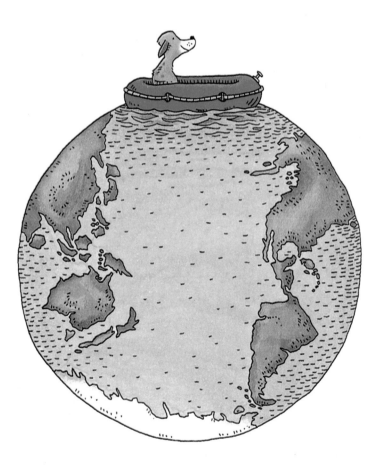

STARFISH BAY
CHILDREN'S BOOKS

Here you can see a doggy crew,
All brave and brilliant – just like you!

Their captain was a dog named Olly,
And he was always bright and jolly.

Although he wasn't the biggest hound,
Life was fun with him around.

One day at the seaside Olly saw
A rubber dinghy on the shore.

"Look, there's a boat!" he cried with glee.
"Now we can sail across the sea!

Come with me, hip hip hooray!
Off we go to the USA!

What? Are you frightened of the unknown?
Then you stay here and I'll sail alone."

And so away he began to float,
Sitting still in his rubber boat.

The wind was blowing loud and strong,
But then a strange bird came along.

"Get out!" howled Olly. "Go away,
And don't come back another day!

I'm the captain. Is that clear?
Passengers aren't wanted here!"

The seagull laughed and said, "OK,
Since you're the captain, I'll give way.

But when I've gone, you'll wish I'd stayed,
Because of the bad mistake you've made."

Then Olly also laughed, looked cool,
And said, "Goodbye, you feathered fool."

What happened next was a big surprise:
The front of the boat began to rise,

And the back of the boat, with Olly in it,
Sank in less than half a minute.

One moment Olly was dry and sailing,
Then suddenly he was wet and wailing.

This was not what he had planned.
Why had he ever left the land?

Water, water, everywhere.
It really was too much to bear.

The sea was deep, his legs were short,
And nowhere could they find support.

The fact was, if he couldn't swim,
This would be the end of him.

Then down he went, down, down and down.
Was Olly now about to drown?

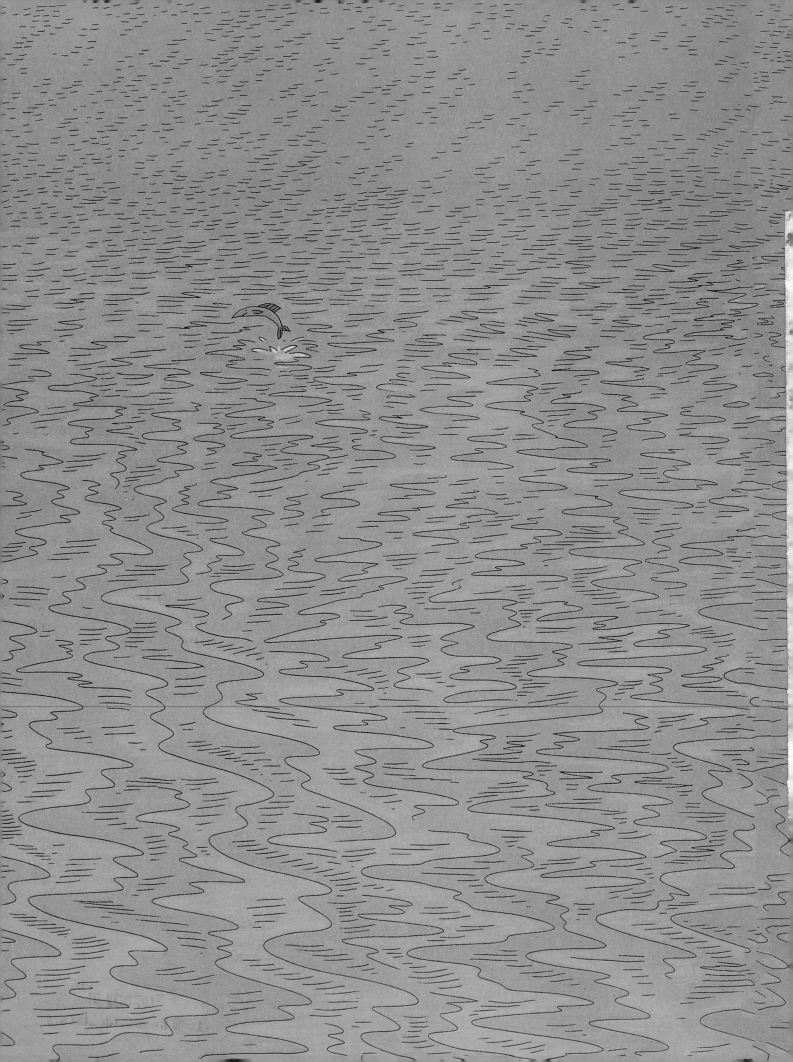

He pumped his legs with might and main,
And at last he reached the top again.

He pumped and paddled till once more
He could see his friends on the sandy shore.

They cheered him home. "Hip hip hooray!
And what was it like in the USA?"